FROM THE FILMS OF **Harry Potter**™ AND **FANTASTIC BEASTS**™

Calling All Witches!

The **Girls** Who **Left Their Mark** on the **Wizarding World**

By **Laurie Calkhoven**   Illustrated by **Violet Tobacco**

SCHOLASTIC INC.

ISBN 978-1-338-32297-2

10 9 8 7 6 5 4 3 2 1   19 20 21 22 23

Printed in Germany 172 • First edition 2019 • Designed by Betsy Peterschmidt

TABLE OF CONTENTS

Calling all

The films of Harry Potter and Fantastic Beasts are filled with witches who rock— brilliant, creative, brave, powerful, and, sometimes, evil women who not only made things happen but also changed the wizarding world forever.

It was Lily Potter's sacrifice, her magic that caused Lord Voldemort's curse to backfire, ridding the world of the Dark Lord for fourteen years. As Ron Weasley puts it in *Harry Potter and the Deathly Hallows – Part 1*, he and Harry Potter wouldn't last "two days" without Hermione Granger, the brightest witch of her age.

Witches!

And as we see in *Fantastic Beasts and Where to Find Them*, without the quick thinking and incredible Legilimency of Queenie Goldstein, Newt Scamander and Tina Goldstein may have been executed before they could expose the Dark wizard Gellert Grindelwald.

But even beyond the heroines we all know and love, there are many examples of witches who were mentors, founders, rule-breakers, mothers, innovators, criminals, professors, and leaders who shaped the wizarding world throughout the films. These are their stories!

Hermione Granger

INTELLIGENT · GIFTED · BRAVE

"You really are the brightest witch of your age."
—Sirius Black, *Harry Potter and the Prisoner of Azkaban*

Every Wizarding World fan knows Hermione Granger—destroyer of Horcruxes, founder of Dumbledore's Army, brightest witch of her age. It was lucky for the wizarding world that Hermione walked into Harry and Ron's train compartment on the Hogwarts Express in *Harry Potter and the Sorcerer's Stone*, as Lord Voldemort likely never would have been defeated without her.

Hermione had a love of learning and a sharp mind that could puzzle out solutions to problems, often before either of her friends. She read everything she could about magic, spending much of her time in the library just for the fun of studying new things. At Hogwarts, one might think that such an intelligent young witch would be sorted into Ravenclaw, but Hermione's courage and determination placed her in Gryffindor. And Hermione proved the Sorting Hat right, as she threw herself into danger time and time again in defense of what she believed in.

But besides brains and bravery, Hermione was a remarkably gifted witch. Often she performed advanced magic that should have been far beyond her ability—especially surprising to some witches and wizards because Hermione was born to non-magical, or Muggle, parents. For this reason, many witches and wizards looked down on her, but Hermione paid them little mind. Hermione had a world to save, and she didn't care what anyone thought about it.

Eight Times Hermione Came to the Rescue

1. In *Harry Potter and the Sorcerer's Stone,* Neville Longbottom did his best to keep Hermione, Ron, and Harry from wandering the castle at night and losing points for Gryffindor. Hermione's response? *"Petrificus Totalus!"* She paralysed Neville and saved the mission.

2. In her second year, Hermione discovered that the Basilisk in the Chamber of Secrets was using the pipes to traverse the castle. She quickly scribbled the word "pipes" on a piece of parchment before being Petrified by the giant snake. Without Hermione's note, Harry might not have found the Chamber in time to save Ginny Weasley.

3. During her third year at Hogwarts, Hermione was able to be in two places at once! In *Harry Potter and the Prisoner of Azkaban,* Hermione used her Time-Turner to go back and save not only Sirius Black, but also Buckbeak the Hippogriff.

4. When Lord Voldemort returned and Professor Umbridge wouldn't properly teach Defense Against the Dark Arts, Hermione had the idea to create Dumbledore's Army so the students could learn defensive spells from one another. Later, the members of Dumbledore's Army used the spells they learned to triumph over the Dark Lord's followers in the Battle of Hogwarts.

HERMIONE GRANGER

5. In *Harry Potter and the Half-Blood Prince*, Hermione knew that Romilda Vane fancied Harry and warned him that Romilda was planning to slip him a love potion. When a box of chocolates from Romilda showed up in Harry's room, Harry knew exactly whom they'd come from and what was inside. (Unfortunately, Ron did not.)

6. In *Harry Potter and the Deathly Hallows – Part 1* and *2*, Hermione used an Undetectable Extension Charm to pack all the things she and her friends needed in one small bag as they searched for Lord Voldemort's Horcruxes. Hermione's planning kept the team going for nearly a year!

7. And when Lord Voldemort's Snatchers came close enough to smell Hermione's perfume, it was Hermione's protective enchantments that kept her team hidden! The Snatchers never figured out that she was standing right in front of them.

8. Destroying Horcruxes is a dangerous business, but in *Harry Potter and the Deathly Hallows – Part 2*, Hermione entered the Chamber of Secrets and used a Basilisk fang to destroy Helga Hufflepuff's cup, one of Lord Voldemort's Horcruxes.

Hermione:
Brilliant on the Fly

─┼─ In her first year, Hermione used the *Alohomora* spell to unlock the door in the third-floor corridor, saving her and her friends from being caught by Filch and also discovering Fluffy, the three-headed dog guarding a trap door.

─┼─ Also in *Harry Potter and the Sorcerer's Stone*, it was Hermione's study of Herbology that helped her identify the Devil's Snare plant and use the *Lumos Solem* spell to free Ron from its grasp.

─┼─ By casting *Finite Incantatem* during a Quidditch match in *Harry Potter and the Chamber of Secrets*, Hermione blew up a rogue Bludger that nearly killed Harry.

HERMIONE GRANGER

—¦— And then there's that time Hermione punched Malfoy in the face! In *Harry Potter and the Prisoner of Azkaban*, Malfoy's lies brought a death sentence down on Buckbeak the Hippogriff. Draco Malfoy was celebrating his triumph when Hermione stood up to him.

—¦— In *Harry Potter and the Deathly Hallows – Part 1*, Ron got Splinched while the trio was Apparating. Not only did Hermione know that essence of dittany would heal him, she had some in her bag!

—¦— It was Hermione's brilliant idea to fly a Ukrainian Ironbelly dragon out of Gringotts Wizarding Bank in *Harry Potter and the Deathly Hallows – Part 2* . . . and she did it with a Horcrux in tow!

Seven Times Hermione Overcame Obstacles

"It's sort of exciting, isn't it? Breaking the rules."

—Hermione Granger, *Harry Potter and the Order of the Phoenix*

1. Some witches and wizards, like Malfoy, didn't like Hermione because her parents were Muggles. They called her "Mudblood," a terrible word for someone who comes from non-magical parents, but as Hagrid says in *Harry Potter and the Chamber of Secrets*, who your parents are doesn't really matter: "They've yet to think of a spell that our Hermione can't do."

2. In her second year, Hermione brewed Polyjuice Potion so she and her friends could disguise themselves as Slytherin students, but a misstep with the ingredients caused her features to change into a cat's. Despite her bad experience, Hermione brewed the potion again, five years later, and broke into Gringotts Wizarding Bank disguised as the Dark witch Bellatrix Lestrange.

3. In *Harry Potter and the Prisoner of Azkaban*, Hermione discovered she wasn't very good at Divination. Although she dropped the class, she later learned to respect the subject when she helped Harry retrieve a prophecy from the Department of Mysteries in *Harry Potter and the Order of the Phoenix*.

4. Although Hermione wanted to go to the Yule Ball with Ron in her fourth year, she accepted an invitation from Durmstrang champion Viktor Krum instead. Ron was being obstinate about asking her, so Hermione decided to put herself first and attend the ball with Krum. Hermione's friendship and diplomacy with Viktor continued for many years, as the pair can be seen dancing at Bill and Fleur's wedding in *Harry Potter and the Deathly Hallows – Part 1*.

5. In *Harry Potter and the Order of the Phoenix*, Hermione organized Dumbledore's Army to convene for their first meeting at the Hog's Head Inn. However, Professor Umbridge issued Educational Decree No. 68, banning all student organizations. Hermione wasn't discouraged though. Dumbledore's Army got creative and moved their lessons to the Room of Requirement.

6. When Lord Voldemort was closing in on his enemies, Hermione used the *Obliviate* spell on her parents. By casting this spell, she erased herself from their memories; she then used magic to erase herself from their family photos. This kept the Grangers protected against the Dark Lord and his Death Eaters, who might have interrogated them.

7. In that same film, *Harry Potter and the Deathly Hallows – Part 1*, Hermione was tortured by Bellatrix Lestrange, who wanted information about the Sword of Gryffindor, but Hermione didn't talk!

Luna Lovegood

CREATIVE · OPEN-MINDED · INDEPENDENT

> **"The things we lose have a way of coming back to us in the end. If not always in the way we expect."**
> —Luna Lovegood, *Harry Potter and the Order of the Phoenix*

In a world filled with all kinds of eccentric witches and wizards, Luna Lovegood stood out from the crowd. This creative witch took her own approach to everything she did, whether she was feeding Thestrals or facing down Death Eaters.

Other students teased her for being different, even calling her "Loony Lovegood," but Luna took it all in stride. An independent witch, her focus never strayed from the things that were most important to her, even when no one else knew what she was talking about.

Luna was incredibly kind and open-minded when it came to new people and new ideas. She grew up in the household that published *The Quibbler*, so she was always fascinated by ideas outside the mainstream. And when it came to lesser known creatures like Nargles and Wrackspurts, Luna was an expert.

This Ravenclaw fiercely defended her ideals and those she cared about—she fought alongside the Order of the Phoenix and was even taken captive by Death Eaters. For all her bravery in battle, however, Luna was perhaps first and foremost renowned for her incredible creativity, her open-mindedness, and her fierce independence.

Six Times Luna Broke the Mold

"You're just as sane as I am."

—Luna Lovegood, *Harry Potter and the Order of the Phoenix*

1. Although most people couldn't see Thestrals or were afraid of their otherworldly appearance, Luna would feed them, as seen in *Harry Potter and the Order of the Phoenix*. When Dumbledore's Army needed to get to the Ministry of Magic fast, Luna relied on her relationship with the creatures to fly her friends to London!

2. Luna had the uncanny ability to find the right words in any situation. Harry was about to leave Dumbledore's Army after some members pressed him for details about Cedric Diggory's death, but Luna stopped him by asking about his Patronus Charm instead. By getting Harry to stay, Luna saved Dumbledore's Army.

3. At the end of the school year in *Harry Potter and the Order of the Phoenix*, Luna searched the castle for her belongings instead of going to the final feast. Although most people might have been upset that other students had hidden her things, Luna said it was all in good fun.

4. In *Harry Potter and the Half-Blood Prince*, Luna used her Spectrespecs to find an unconscious Harry in Draco Malfoy's compartment on the Hogwarts Express. She wore the strange glasses because she was hoping to see Wrackspurts—invisible creatures who float into a person's ears and cause confusion—but found Harry instead!

5. Despite being a Ravenclaw, Luna crafted an intricate Gryffindor lion's head, which she wore to support Ron in his first Quidditch match in *Harry Potter and the Half-Blood Prince.*

6. Many students were unkind to the Grey Lady, but Luna took time to befriend the ghost, who was, in fact, Helena Ravenclaw. Thanks to the trust Helena placed in Luna, she agreed to speak to Harry, leading him to the Lost Diadem of Ravenclaw in *Harry Potter and the Deathly Hallows – Part 2.*

Ginny Weasley

"Leave him alone!"

—Ginny Weasley, *Harry Potter and the Chamber of Secrets*

As the youngest in a wizarding family with six older brothers, learning to be gutsy was a necessity . . . and "gutsy" is exactly the word to describe Ginny Weasley. Ginny's brothers sometimes brushed her off as a *little* sister, but Ginny proved over and over again that she was a force to be reckoned with.

In *Harry Potter and the Chamber of Secrets*, Ginny got off to a rocky start in her first year at Hogwarts when Lucius Malfoy slipped Tom Riddle's diary in with her school books at Flourish and Blotts. The diary turned out to be a Horcrux, and it took over Ginny's mind, forcing her to open the Chamber of Secrets. She not only freed the Basilisk inside but also terrorized the school with threatening messages written in blood. Tom Riddle (also known as Lord Voldemort) was about to sacrifice Ginny to make himself stronger when Harry destroyed the diary with the Basilisk's fang and saved her life at the last moment.

That was the last time Ginny needed to be saved. She proved herself to be both a strong and fierce competitor on the Quidditch pitch as Gryffindor's star Chaser. And, as a member of Dumbledore's Army, Ginny was not afraid to stand up to anybody—even Death Eaters.

Eight Times Ginny Took Charge

1. Ginny might have been a first year, but she wasn't afraid to stand up to Draco Malfoy in Flourish and Blotts in *Harry Potter and the Chamber of Secrets*.

2. Ginny shocked everyone the first time she cast the Reducto Curse in training with Dumbledore's Army. She blasted a Dark wizard dummy into little bits in *Harry Potter and the Order of the Phoenix*.

3. In her fourth year, Ginny jumped on a Thestral to fly to the Department of Mysteries alongside Dumbledore's Army—even though the creature was invisible to her. She put her D.A. training to the test at the Ministry, where she held her own in a battle with Death Eaters.

4. No one seemed to pay much mind to Harry at Quidditch tryouts in *Harry Potter and the Half-Blood Prince*. Luckily, Ginny silenced everyone with a quick, "Shut it!"

5. Ginny also knew when to tell people to back off. When Fred, George, and Ron took an interest in Ginny's love life in *Harry Potter and the Half-Blood Prince*, Ginny let her brothers know that whom she dated was none of their business.

6. That same year, Ginny convinced Harry to give up the Half-Blood Prince's book after a spell he found inside it went awry. Ginny, after all, knew better than anyone the kind of damage a book could do.

7. Life at Hogwarts wasn't exactly *pleasant* in *Harry Potter and the Deathly Hallows – Part 1* and *2*, with Professor Snape as headmaster and the Death Eaters teaching classes. But Ginny worked with Neville to organize the remaining Hogwarts students and re-form Dumbledore's Army.

8. During the Battle of Hogwarts, Ginny dueled the Death Eaters alongside her mother, coming face-to-face with the most dangerous of Dark witches, Bellatrix Lestrange.

WITCHES HAVE YOUR BACK!

When the going got tough, these witches were looking out for one another. Whether they were cheering on a friend's accomplishments or watching out for a sister or defending someone who was once a rival, witches stick together.

-|- When Dolores Umbridge fired Divination Professor Sybill Trelawney in *Harry Potter and the Order of the Phoenix*, Professor McGonagall defended and comforted the distraught teacher.

-|- When Ron tried to make light of Cho Chang's emotions in *Harry Potter and the Order of the Phoenix*, Hermione quickly silenced him by explaining the tremendous pressure Cho was under and the complicated emotions that Cho was feeling about Harry.

-|- It was Luna's friendship with the Grey Lady, Helena Ravenclaw, that convinced the ghost to reveal where her mother's diadem—one of Lord Voldemort's Horcruxes—was located.

- Despite their rocky history, Hermione attempted to save Lavender Brown, Ron Weasley's ex-girlfriend, by cursing the dangerous werewolf Fenrir Greyback during the Battle of Hogwarts.

- In *Harry Potter and the Goblet of Fire*, when Fleur Delacour, representing the French magical school, Beauxbatons, was selected to compete as champion in the Triwizard Tournament, her fellow classmates cheered her on.

- Although not a witch, it was clear that Petunia Evans (later Dursley) loved her sister, Lily—though she had conflicted feelings about Lily's magic and her marriage to James. After Lily's death, Petunia could not find it in her to turn away her sister's orphaned infant son, Harry.

- When Bellatrix Lestrange was concerned that her sister, Narcissa Malfoy, put her trust in the wrong person (Severus Snape), she made Snape take an Unbreakable Vow to protect "Cissy's" family at all costs.

THE WOMEN OF DUMBLEDORE'S ARMY

"We've got to be able to defend ourselves, and if Umbridge refuses to teach us how, we need someone who will."

—Hermione Granger, *Harry Potter and the Order of the Phoenix*

Cho Chang

RESILIENT

Cho Chang, an intelligent and curious Ravenclaw, was one of the most resilient characters of the Wizarding World film series. After her first love, Cedric Diggory, was murdered by Lord Voldemort in *Harry Potter and the Goblet of Fire*, Cho joined Dumbledore's Army and worked hard to master defensive spells like the Patronus Charm. (Her Patronus took the shape of a swan.)

Cho's membership in the D.A. was especially dangerous, considering that Professor Umbridge was trying to have her mother fired from the Ministry of Magic.

Cho and Harry shared a first kiss but broke up after Professor Umbridge used Veritaserum, a powerful truth potion, to force Cho to reveal where Dumbledore's Army met. But in *Harry Potter and the Deathly Hallows – Part 2*, Cho still rallied to the organization's side when she battled Death Eaters during the Battle of Hogwarts.

Lavender Brown

PROTECTIVE

Lavender Brown had a huge heart, and once a person won her over, she was in their corner forever. Lavender was sorted into Gryffindor the same year as Harry, Ron, and Hermione. She was a favorite of Divination Professor Sybill Trelawney and grew especially angry when Dolores Umbridge fired her.

In *Harry Potter and the Half-Blood Prince*, Lavender was a member of Dumbledore's Army and briefly dated Ron. When Ron was accidentally poisoned in Professor Slughorn's office, Lavender rushed to his side only to find Hermione there first. A nasty breakup followed, but that didn't stop Lavender from joining the battle against the Dark Lord in *Harry Potter and the Deathly Hallows – Part 2*.

Parvati Patil

OUTGOING

Parvati Patil was close friends with Lavender Brown; they shared a love for Divination. Parvati had a flair for passing notes, she even helped send a clue to Harry about the first task of the Triwizard Tournament.

In her fourth year, Parvati accepted an invitation to the Yule Ball from Harry Potter. Harry was a pretty bad date, which is why Parvati ditched him halfway through the night to dance with her friends. Parvati still volunteered to fight alongside and learn some new spells from Harry when she joined Dumbledore's Army a year later.

Padma Patil

Parvati's twin, Padma, mastered defensive spells in Dumbledore's Army and was always the first to cheer the accomplishments of her fellow classmates. She also survived a terrible date to the Yule Ball with Ron in *Harry Potter and the Goblet of Fire*. Padma was a fierce warrior in the Battle of Hogwarts, and when it was all over, she congregated with fellow students Katie, Cho, and Leanne for support.

Susan Bones

FAIR

Hufflepuff Susan Bones joined Professor Gilderoy Lockhart's Dueling Club, which was formed after the first Basilisk attack in *Harry Potter and the Chamber of Secrets*. That club's first meeting was also its last.

But that little snafu didn't stop Susan from joining Dumbledore's Army. Like the other D.A. members, she wanted to learn everything Harry had to teach about Disarming Charms, Dementors, and Death Eaters. She used what she learned in the Battle of Hogwarts, defending her school and her friends against Lord Voldemort's forces.

Hannah Abbott

Hufflepuff Hannah Abbott always stood up for what was right. She defended Harry in *Harry Potter and the Chamber of Secrets* when other students claimed he was a Dark wizard because he was a Parselmouth. She was also one of the first members of Dumbledore's Army. Sadly, Hannah left school when her mother was murdered by Death Eaters, but she returned to join the revived Dumbledore's Army led by Ginny and Luna in *Harry Potter and the Deathly Hallows – Part 1* and *2*.

SERIOUS SPELLWORK

Members of Dumbledore's Army had to master all kinds of spells as they learned how to battle Death Eaters and Dark creatures.

- *Expelliarmus!* This Disarming Charm forces an opponent to drop his or her wand.

- *Stupefy!* Cho Chang mastered the Stunning Spell, which leaves a victim unconscious—at least until it wears off!

- *Levicorpus!* This spell leaves its victim suspended in midair. Luna Lovegood used this spell on a Death Eater in the battle at the Department of Mysteries after learning it in a D.A. meeting.

- *Reducto!* Ginny Weasley shocked her brothers with the force of her Reductor Curse, which splits solid objects into tiny pieces.

- *Expecto Patronum!* The Patronus Charm, which repels Dementors, is one of the most difficult spells to master, but Luna, Cho, Ginny, and Hermione were all able to conjure a full-bodied Patronus in a D.A. meeting.

Myrtle Warren

FIERY · CANDID · DETERMINED

"If you die down there, you're welcome to share my toilet."
—Myrtle Warren, *Harry Potter and the Chamber of Secrets*

Myrtle Warren, also known as Moaning Myrtle, was the fiery ghost who haunted the Hogwarts girls' bathroom. Once an intelligent Muggle-born Ravenclaw, Myrtle was also a sensitive young woman who was bullied by another student, Olive Hornby. Fifty years before the events of *Harry Potter and the Chamber of Secrets*, Myrtle was crying in the bathroom over her ill treatment when she was murdered by Tom Riddle, who commanded Slytherin's Basilisk to kill her.

Myrtle didn't take insults well; she was determined to have the respect she deserved. After Ron claimed it shouldn't matter that someone had thrown a book at her, because it couldn't hurt her, Myrtle retorted, "Oh sure! Let's all throw books at Myrtle because she can't feel it!"

THREE TIMES MYRTLE SAVED THE DAY

1. Myrtle's habit of moaning and flooding the girls' bathroom whenever she had a tantrum kept most students away, but not Hermione! Thanks to Myrtle, Hermione had the perfect place to brew Polyjuice Potion in *Harry Potter and the Chamber of Secrets*.

2. By sharing the story of her death with Harry, Myrtle helped him find the entrance to the Chamber of Secrets, effectively saving Ginny Weasley's life and destroying the very Horcrux Lord Voldemort had created through Myrtle's death. Top that for a tale of sweet revenge!

3. Myrtle came to the rescue again in *Harry Potter and the Goblet of Fire* when she appeared in the prefects' bathroom to give Harry some information about how to open the golden egg that contained the clue to his second Triwizard Tournament task.

GIRLS WHO RULED THE QUIDDITCH PITCH

Ginny Weasley wasn't the only witch at Hogwarts who loved Quidditch. Many girls were fierce competitors on and off the field!

Katie Bell

TOUGH

"I know Katie. Off the Quidditch pitch she wouldn't hurt a fly."
—Harry Potter, *Harry Potter and the Half-Blood Prince*

Another talented Chaser on the Gryffindor Quidditch team, Katie Bell showed an interest in Defense Against the Dark Arts early on, joining the Dueling Club in *Harry Potter and the Chamber of Secrets* and then Dumbledore's Army in *Harry Potter and the Order of the Phoenix*.

The Gryffindor was lucky to survive after Malfoy cast the Imperius Curse on her in *Harry Potter and the Half-Blood Prince*. The spell—one of the three Unforgivable Curses—placed her under Malfoy's control. He forced Katie to take a cursed opal necklace to Dumbledore, but the package containing the necklace tore, and Katie touched it instead. This tough girl survived and was back in class after the winter break.

Angelina Johnson

DIPLOMATIC

"Angelina Johnson scores! Ten points for Gryffindor!"
—Lee Jordan, *Harry Potter and the Sorcerer's Stone*

A top member of the Gryffindor Quidditch team, Angelina Johnson was a hard-hitting Chaser who excelled at getting the Quaffle through the goal hoop. Angelina could be seen leading her fellow Chasers on the field, scoring goal after goal in the Slytherin matches in her second and third years. In *Harry Potter and the Goblet of Fire*, she threw her name in for the Triwizard Tournament, but when she wasn't selected, she supported fellow Gryffindor Harry Potter.

Alicia Spinnet

ACTIVE

Like Angelina Johnson and Katie Bell, Alicia Spinnet was a Chaser on the Gryffindor team when Harry was a Seeker. And like the others, she joined Dumbledore's Army and came to the school's defense when Lord Voldemort and his Death Eaters attacked. No doubt Alicia's expert moves on the Quidditch pitch served her well during the Battle of Hogwarts.

MAJOR QUIDDITCH MOMENTS

In *Harry Potter and the Sorcerer's Stone*, Angelina Johnson flew alongside Harry in his first game as Seeker. She scored twenty points for Gryffindor early in the game. Later she was boxed in by two Slytherins, who ran her into the stands. Angelina never let the Slytherin team's dirty tricks turn her away from the sport, though.

In *Harry Potter and the Half-Blood Prince*, Ginny Weasley stepped up to run the Gryffindor team tryouts. Ginny was a double threat, taking up the positions of Chaser and Seeker in different games.

Ginny was at it again during their game against Slytherin, scoring ten points after outmaneuvering the Slytherin Keeper, causing him to fall off his broomstick.

In that same game from *Harry Potter and the Half-Blood Prince*, Alicia can be seen tearing apart Slytherin's tight formation as they approach the goal hoops, setting up a nice save for the Gryffindor Keeper.

That wasn't the only time Alicia was on fire though. During a match against Hufflepuff in *Harry Potter and the Prisoner of Azkaban*, her broom was struck by lightning—she was *literally* on fire!

Chaser: The Chaser's job is to score goals by throwing the Quaffle through one of three hoops on the Quidditch pitch. One goal is worth ten points, and each team has three Chasers. Ginny, Alicia, Katie, and Angelina were all fast and agile Chasers.

Keeper: Guarding the team's three goal hoops falls to the Keeper, who must prevent the enemy team from scoring. In *Harry Potter and the Sorcerer's Stone*, Slytherin's Keeper missed two saves, leading Angelina Johnson to score twice.

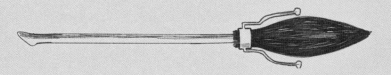

Beater: A Quidditch team has two Beaters, who must keep the two Bludgers away from their teammates by batting them toward the opposing team.

Seeker: The Seeker hunts the Golden Snitch, a small winged ball that flits about the field. Once the Seeker catches the ball, her team scores one hundred and fifty points, ending the game. Cho Chang was a Seeker for the Ravenclaw team!

Fleur Delacour

POISED · DEDICATED · ACCOMPLISHED

"Miss Delacour? She's as much a fairy princess as I am."
—Barty Crouch Jr., disguised as Mad-Eye Moody, *Harry Potter and the Goblet of Fire*

Star student Fleur Delacour captivated the population of Hogwarts from the moment Beauxbatons's blue carriage and its winged horses came into view in *Harry Potter and the Goblet of Fire*. After putting her name in the Goblet of Fire, Fleur easily stepped into her role as the Triwizard Tournament champion representing Beauxbatons.

Long after the Triwizard Tournament was over, Fleur remained dedicated to the Order of the Phoenix. In *Harry Potter and the Deathly Hallows – Part 1*, she put her life on the line to transport Harry Potter to a safe house, drinking Polyjuice Potion to disguise herself as Harry and fighting off Death Eaters with her then-fiancé, Bill Weasley. Her wedding to Bill was cut short when Lord Voldemort took over the Ministry of Magic, and Death Eaters Apparated into the middle of her wedding reception.

Along with the rest of the Weasley family, Fleur answered the call and fought bravely in the Battle of Hogwarts. She may have looked sweet, but that didn't mean she couldn't also duel with Death Eaters.

FLEUR'S THREE TRIWIZARD TOURNAMENT TASKS

1. Fleur easily conjured a sleeping trance to claim her golden egg from a Common Welsh Green dragon in the first Triwizard task.

2. During her second task, Fleur used the Bubble-Head Charm to swim in the Black Lake, though she placed last after being overwhelmed by a swarm of Grindylows.

3. Fleur found her way through an obstacle-filled maze for the tournament's third task but was brutally stunned by Viktor Krum, who was under the Imperius Curse by one of the Dark Lord's followers. Perhaps this is what gave Fleur a taste for fighting Death Eaters!

Madame Olympe Maxime

OPINIONATED · CUNNING · MENTOR

"C'est magnifique!"

—Olympe Maxime, *Harry Potter and the Goblet of Fire*

Olympe Maxime was the elegant headmistress of Beauxbatons Academy of Magic, a wizarding school like Hogwarts that's hidden away in the mountains of France. Madame Maxime escorted her students, including Fleur, to Hogwarts for the Triwizard Tournament in *Harry Potter and the Goblet of Fire*. She made sure her concerns were heard when Hogwarts got two champions in the tournament, where Beauxbatons only had one.

As a half-giantess, Madame Maxime immediately attracted Hagrid's attention, especially after she asked him to care for Beauxbatons's winged horses. She charmed Hagrid into granting her a peek at the dragons that the Triwizard champions would face in the first task, giving Beauxbatons an edge in the competition.

While she was very focused on mentoring Fleur, her young Triwizard champion, Madame Maxime did take at least one night off to dance with Hagrid at the Yule Ball; however, this headmistress didn't really have time for romance. She had students to chaperone and a champion to support!

Professor Minerva McGonagall

PROUD · WISE · WATCHFUL

"Gryffindor has commanded the respect of the wizard world for nearly ten centuries. I will not have you in the course of a single evening besmirching that name."

—Minerva McGonagall, *Harry Potter and the Goblet of Fire*

Hermione Granger might have been the most brilliant student at Hogwarts during her time, but Minerva McGonagall likely would have given Hermione a run for her Galleons. McGonagall held various posts at Hogwarts, including Transfiguration professor and the Head of Gryffindor house, before ascending to headmistress.

As a member of the Order of the Phoenix, McGonagall kept her status in the organization a secret, preferring to do her part behind the scenes. She showed time and again that her first loyalty was to Hogwarts and its students. In *Harry Potter and the Goblet of Fire*, she had sharp words for Snape and Dumbledore when they suggested using Harry as bait for whatever plan the Death Eaters had in store, remarking, "Well the devil with Barty [Crouch] and his rules! And since when did you accommodate the Ministry? . . . Potter is a boy! Not a piece of meat!"

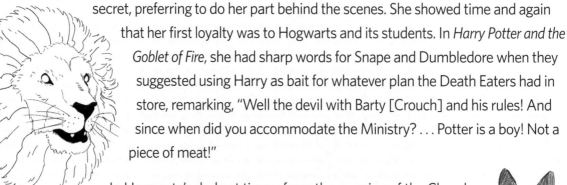

In Hogwarts's darkest times, from the opening of the Chamber of Secrets to the death of Cedric Diggory, even as the school was overtaken first by the Ministry and later by Lord Voldemort, McGonagall remained a constant, powerful magical force. She was always the first to defend her students and staff when they needed protection—and the first to lend them a sharp correction when they were out of line.

FIVE TIMES
MCGONAGALL BROKE THE RULES

Professor McGonagall was a strict teacher who didn't put up
with nonsense in her classes, and she didn't hesitate to take points from her own house,
Gryffindor, when she thought Harry, Ron, and Hermione had broken the rules. That said, she
wasn't above breaking the rules herself from time to time.

1. Tired of Slytherin's repeated Quidditch victories, McGonagall saw Harry's skillful (if unlawful) flying in *Harry Potter and the Sorcerer's Stone* and appointed him Seeker on the Gryffindor Quidditch team.

2. While none of the other teachers seemed willing to talk about the Chamber of Secrets, McGonagall leveled with her students, telling them all about the founders of Hogwarts and the mythic forbidden chamber hidden somewhere in the school.

3. In *Harry Potter and the Prisoner of Azkaban*, McGonagall gave Hermione a Time-Turner so that she could attend extra classes.

4. McGonagall did what she could to rebel against the Ministry of Magic in *Harry Potter and the Order the Phoenix*, questioning Dolores Umbridge's medieval policies at every turn and comforting her colleague, Professor Trelawney, when she was fired.

5. In *Harry Potter and the Deathly Hallows – Part 2*, when Harry confronted Severus Snape in the Great Hall, McGonagall shoved Harry out of the way and dueled the then-headmaster into a corner. She chased him from the castle and then called on Hogwarts's allies as well as the castle's enchanted armor to battle the Dark Lord in defense of the school.

FIVE TIMES
MCGONAGALL WARNED YOU

"Hogwarts is threatened! Man the boundaries!"
—Minerva McGonagall, *Harry Potter and the Goblet of Fire*

1. In *Harry Potter and the Sorcerer's Stone*, McGonagall cautioned Dumbledore not to leave Harry with the Dursleys. "They're the worst kind of Muggles," she said.

2. Before the Sorting Ceremony, McGonagall warned all first years that any rule breaking would lose them house points. She was right; when Harry, Ron, and Hermione took their chances and went out after dark, they lost fifty points each for Gryffindor.

3. When Ron's wand broke as a result of the flying car crashing into the Whomping Willow, McGonagall warned him that it needed replacing. Later, when Ron tried to use it to hit Draco Malfoy with a Slug-Vomiting Charm for insulting Hermione, his curse backfired, causing Ron to vomit up slugs.

4. McGonagall wasn't afraid to stand up to Dumbledore. In *Harry Potter and the Goblet of Fire*, she warned the headmaster that only trouble would follow if Harry entered the Triwizard Tournament—and she was right!

5. In that same film, McGonagall tried to teach her students to dance for the Yule Ball. She warned Harry that he'd have to open the ball with the other champions. Harry didn't listen, of course, and was shocked when he arrived with Parvati and had to dance with her!

Professor Sybill Trelawney

INTUITIVE · CURIOUS · GIFTED

> **"The truth lies buried, like a sentence deep within a book, waiting to be read. But first, you must broaden your minds."**
>
> —Sybill Trelawney, *Harry Potter and the Prisoner of Azkaban*

Professor Sybill Trelawney taught Divination at Hogwarts during the majority of Harry, Ron, and Hermione's time there. Although many students (mostly Hermione) doubted her craft, Trelawney was a sometimes-talented Seer who prophesied the Dark Lord's return in *Harry Potter and the Prisoner of Azkaban*. But when she wasn't making accurate predictions, Professor Trelawney liked to say that her students (mostly Harry) were going to die.

When Dolores Umbridge took over Hogwarts in *Harry Potter and the Order of the Phoenix*, she challenged Sybill to come up with a prediction on the spot and fired her when she couldn't. Despite being dismissed from her position, Professors McGonagall and Dumbledore came to Trelawney's defense and allowed her to live at Hogwarts even if she couldn't teach there.

Professor Trelawney participated in the Battle of Hogwarts in *Harry Potter and the Deathly Hallows – Part 2*, fighting Death Eaters in the ensuing battle and tending to those who were injured in the Great Hall.

TWO TIMES PROFESSOR TRELAWNEY'S PREDICTIONS CAME TRUE

1. In *Harry Potter and the Prisoner of Azkaban*, Sybill fell into a trance and predicted that one of the Dark Lord's servants would be freed and reunited with his master. That very night, Ron's rat, Scabbers, was revealed to be Peter Pettigrew, the man who told Lord Voldemort where Harry's parents lived, resulting in their deaths. Pettigrew escaped Harry and helped the Dark Lord return to power.

2. In *Harry Potter and the Order of the Phoenix*, Lord Voldemort lured Harry to the Department of Mysteries to collect a prophecy that was created by none other than Trelawney herself! The prophecy revealed that Harry would have to kill—or be killed by—the Dark Lord, "for neither can live while the other survives."

Professor Pomona Sprout

KNOWLEDGEABLE · HUMBLE · FAIR-MINDED

> "As I understand it, Madam Sprout has a very healthy growth of Mandrakes, and when matured, a potion will be made which will revive Mrs. Norris."
>
> —Albus Dumbledore, *Harry Potter and the Chamber of Secrets*

Professor Pomona Sprout was Hogwarts' Herbology professor and also the Head of Hufflepuff house. Her extensive knowledge served her well in her profession, teaching students all about the care and keeping of magical plants. Her Devil's Snare plant was one of the enchantments guarding the Sorcerer's Stone during Harry's first year at Hogwarts. Hermione only knew how to defeat it because she had paid attention in Professor Sprout's class.

As the Head of Hufflepuff, she was exceedingly humble and fair-minded, lending her talents without hesitation to the Order of the Phoenix during the Battle of Hogwarts. After Death Eaters shattered the protective spells around Hogwarts, Professor Sprout's plants were seen bringing down Lord Voldemort's giants as they rushed the castle. She tended to the wounded as well, and after the battle, she was seen enjoying a cup of tea with Professors Flitwick and Slughorn in *Harry Potter and the Deathly Hallows – Part 2*.

PROFESSOR SPROUT TO THE RESCUE!

In *Harry Potter and the Chamber of Secrets*, Professor Sprout nurtured a growth of Mandrake plants through to adulthood. The plants looked like very ugly babies, but when they were grown they could be used to create a Restorative Draught that could cure Petrification. After the Basilisk Petrified three students, a ghost, and a cat at Hogwarts, Professor Sprout's Mandrake Restorative Draught saved all of them!

Madam Poppy Pomfrey

QUICK · CONFIDENT · SKILLED

"I can mend bones in a heartbeat, but growing them back? . . . Regrowing bones is a nasty business."

—Poppy Pomfrey, *Harry Potter and the Chamber of Secrets*

Students were taken into the skilled care of Hogwarts's school matron, Madam Pomfrey, with all sorts of creative injuries—and it took a healer equally creative to get them back on their feet. Whether she had to regrow Harry's bones after a spell gone wrong, cure Hermione after she gave herself fur and a tail with Polyjuice Potion, or treat Ron after he drank poisoned mead, this school nurse was always confident and quick thinking in her treatments. And when she said rest, she *meant* it!

Madam Pomfrey, alongside Professor Sprout, played an integral role in healing all those Petrified by the Basilisk in *Harry Potter and the Chamber of Secrets*. The Mandrake Draught may have been somewhat easy to administer to Hermione, Colin, Justin, and Mrs. Norris, but one can only imagine what it took to un-Petrify a ghost like Nearly Headless Nick!

Protective of her students—both the injured and the healthy—Madam Pomfrey fought and healed alongside them and their professors in the Battle of Hogwarts.

Madam Irma Pince

ORDERLY

If Madam Pomfrey kept a tight watch on Hogwarts' students, Madam Pince kept an even tighter watch on the library. Only it wasn't the students she was protecting, it was the books! The Hogwarts librarian frowned on food, talking, laughing, whispering, sneezing, and any other activities that might disturb the peace of the library or her precious books.

Still, some of Hogwarts's greatest and most terrible finds came out of Madam Pince's library. It was here in *Harry Potter and the Chamber of Secrets* that Hermione worked out how to brew Polyjuice Potion and how the Basilisk was traversing Hogwarts. But it was also in the library where the future Lord Voldemort first read about Horcruxes.

Madam Hooch

COMMANDING

"Now I want a nice, clean game . . . from all of you!"

—Madam Hooch, *Harry Potter and the Sorcerer's Stone*

Hogwarts's flying instructor and Quidditch referee Madam Hooch introduced first years to flying in *Harry Potter and the Sorcerer's Stone*. A commanding but compassionate teacher, Madam Hooch took Neville Longbottom into her care when he fell off his broomstick and broke his wrist during the students' first flying lesson.

In that same lesson, Harry proved adept at flying, although his brilliant first flight broke Madam Hooch's own rules about flying unsupervised. Still, it seems Madam Hooch was never the wiser to Harry's forbidden flight.

Madam Hooch was the referee of Harry's first Quidditch match against Slytherin. When Harry caught the Snitch, she was the first to gleefully announce, "Gryffindor wins!"

Professor Wilhelmina Grubbly-Plank

SUPPORTIVE

Professor Grubbly-Plank joined Hogwarts' staff in *Harry Potter and the Order of the Phoenix* as the Care of Magical Creatures professor while Hagrid was on a mission for Dumbledore, trying to get the Giants to join in their fight against Lord Voldemort. She was quick to stand up for Dumbledore when questioned by Dolores Umbridge and later on did her best to protect her students from the sinister headmistress.

Professor Charity Burbage

TOLERANT

Professor Burbage taught Muggle Studies at Hogwarts. She believed that Muggles were not all that different from witches and wizards, and that Muggle-borns were just as worthy of a magical education as pure-blood wizards. Unfortunately, her editorial in *The Daily Prophet* promoting her views drew Lord Voledmort's attention. She was held captive and tortured at Malfoy Manor, where she begged her friend Severus Snape for his help. The Dark Lord murdered her for her beliefs, but Professor Burbage was remembered for standing up for what was right in the face of evil.

VILLAINS OF THE WIZARDING WORLD

These witches were Bad with a capital "B." They imprisoned, tortured, and murdered many innocent people, all in pursuit of a world where pure-blood witches and wizards could rule over everyone else. But while it's important to learn from our heroes, it can be just as important to learn from the villains who fought them. The witches that follow were magnetic, ambitious, and powerful—all admirable qualities—but they used their gifts in pursuit of some of the most evil aims of the film series. Beware these villains of the Wizarding World!

Dolores Umbridge

"Enough! I will have order!"

—Dolores Umbridge, *Harry Potter and the Order of the Phoenix*

Dolores Umbridge might have used three teaspoons of sugar in her tea, but she was anything but sweet. The Senior Undersecretary to the Minister for Magic took over as Hogwarts's Defense Against the Dark Arts professor in *Harry Potter and the Order of the Phoenix*, but her ambitions led her to climb the ranks to Hogwarts High Inquisitor, and later, after forcing Dumbledore out, headmistress.

When the Ministry was forced to acknowledge that Lord Voldemort had returned, Dolores Umbridge left Hogwarts to return to her former job, but her authoritarian nature ensured she didn't become any less ruthless at enforcing the law—fair or unfair.

Yet the witch believed that she had the right to break the law. In *Harry Potter and the Deathly Hallows – Part 1*, it was discovered that she had taken a locket from a thief as a bribe. That locket, which once belonged to Salazar Slytherin, was one of Lord Voldemort's Horcruxes. It was stolen again by Harry, Ron, and Hermione and destroyed.

Seven Times Dolores Umbridge Was the Worst

1. Umbridge sought Harry's expulsion from Hogwarts during Harry's hearing at the Ministry for casting a Patronus Charm in front of a Muggle (his cousin).

2. She took over as the Defense Against the Dark Arts teacher but refused to teach her students to defend themselves or to use magic in her class.

3. As punishment for speaking about Lord Voldemort's return, she forced Harry to use a special quill that used his blood as ink and scratched messages into his skin.

4. She used Veritaserum, a powerful truth potion, to force students to confess to "illicit" behavior, including Cho Chang, who unwillingly revealed where Dumbledore's Army met in *Harry Potter and the Order of the Phoenix*.

5. She called the Centaurs in the forest "filthy half-breeds."

6. She gave Argus Filch permission to punish students with torture.

7. After she returned to the Ministry, she happily put Muggle-borns on trial and sent them to Azkaban with the lie that they had stolen their wands from "real" witches and wizards.

Alecto Carrow

Alecto Carrow was one of Lord Voldemort's Death Eaters. She was led into Hogwarts castle by Draco Malfoy through his Vanishing Cabinet and was present when Severus Snape killed Dumbledore. Along with her brother, Alecto joined the faculty at Hogwarts after the Ministry fell, having been appointed by then-headmaster Snape, though she still attended meetings at Malfoy Manor, as seen in *Harry Potter and the Deathly Hallows – Part 1*.

At Hogwarts, Alecto's official role was to teach Muggle Studies. But her real role was torturing students—and at that, she excelled. She and her brother tried to force Neville Longbottom and other seventh-year students to practice the Cruciatus Curse to torture first years.

During the Battle of Hogwarts, Alecto was accidentally Stunned by Snape when he was deflecting defensive curses from Minerva McGonagall.

Bellatrix Lestrange

"Oh, he knows how to play, itty-bitty baby Potter."
—Bellaxtrix Lestrange, *Harry Potter and the Order of the Phoenix*

Perhaps Lord Voldemort's most loyal Death Eater, Bellatrix Lestrange took great joy in her evil tasks. An incredibly powerful witch, she delighted in torturing and murdering those she and the Dark Lord deemed inferior.

Unyielding in pursuit of her goals, Bellatrix tortured Neville Longbottom's Auror parents in the First Wizarding War. She escaped from Azkaban prison in *Harry Potter and the Order of Phoenix* and immediately rejoined Lord Voldemort. Her devotion to the Dark wizard was evident; when her nephew Draco was set to carry out her master's bidding, she was bursting with pride.

BELLATRIX'S MOST SINISTER ACTS

- In *Harry Potter and the Order of the Phoenix*, Bellatrix murdered her cousin and Harry's godfather, Sirius Black, while trying to steal a prophecy.

- In *Harry Potter and the Half-Blood Prince*, Bellatrix and the werewolf Fenrir Greyback set the Weasleys' home on fire. All the while she chanted, "I killed Sirius Black!"

- Bellatrix was even more determined to catch Harry in *Harry Potter and the Deathly Hallows – Part 1.* With the help of Snatchers, Harry, Ron, and Hermione ended up at Malfoy Manor, where Bellatrix tortured Hermione to find out how the trio got the Sword of Gryffindor.

- Bellatrix was at the Dark Lord's side during the Battle of Hogwarts, she threw herself into attack after attack until she came across Ginny and Molly Weasley. Just as Bellatrix was about to deliver the Killing Curse upon Ginny, Molly took her out.

TOUGH MOTHERS

By now you've heard about a lot of witches who left their mark, but they wouldn't have got very far without these formidable matriarchs! The witches who follow weren't afraid to fight for a better future and risk everything, all while doing their part to bring up the next generation of heroes.

Alice Longbottom

NOBLE · STRONG · DETERMINED

"Frank and Alice Longbottom . . . they suffered a fate worse than death."
—Sirius Black, *Harry Potter and the Deathly Hallows – Part 2*

Alice Longbottom was an Auror (a Dark wizard catcher), who dedicated her life to protecting the wizarding world from the Dark Arts. She and her husband, Frank, were members of the original Order of the Phoenix, alongside the Potters and the Weasleys. They fought against Lord Voldemort and his Death Eaters during the First Wizarding War.

When Harry's friend Neville Longbottom was just a baby, Bellatrix Lestrange tortured Alice and her husband with the Cruciatus Curse, one of three Unforgivable Curses. Despite her torture, Alice never revealed anything that could be used against the Order.

Throughout Neville's childhood, Alice remained in St. Mungo's Hospital with no hope of recovery. But Neville—and others—were inspired by her strength. About his parents, Neville confided in Harry that he was "Quite proud to be their son."

TOUGH MOTHERS

Lily Potter

KIND · MAGNETIC · ACCOMPLISHED

"Not only was [Lily] a singularly gifted witch, she was also an uncommonly kind woman. She had a way of seeing the beauty in others even, and perhaps most especially, when that person could not see it in themselves."

—Professor Lupin to Harry in *Harry Potter and the Prisoner of Azkaban*

There was always something unusual about Muggle-born Lily Evans. Strange and beautiful things happened around her. One day, a boy named Severus Snape approached Lily. He was from a magical family and knew right away that Lily was a witch. When the two were eleven years old, they started Hogwarts together, where Lily stood up to those who bullied Severus. But their friendship ended when he got involved in the Dark Arts, and she fell in love with James Potter.

Lily was quite an accomplished witch during and after her time at Hogwarts, and was a favorite student of Horace Slughorn. In *Harry Potter and the Half-Blood Prince*, Lily's memory inspired Slughorn to give Harry one of his most guarded secrets—that Slughorn had revealed how to make a Horcrux to a young Lord Voldemort.

In adulthood, Lily married James, and they were among the original members of the Order of the Phoenix when Lord Voldemort rose to power. During the First Wizarding War, Lily, James, and their infant son, Harry, were forced into hiding in Godric's Hollow. After Peter Pettigrew revealed their location, Lily bravely faced Lord Voldemort and sacrificed her life to save her son. Her boundless love protected the infant, causing Lord Voldemort's Killing Curse to rebound. It was old and powerful magic that the Dark Lord had not foreseen. Lily saved the entire wizarding world, though few knew it at the time.

Molly Weasley

FIERCE · PROTECTIVE · JUST

"Just because you're allowed to use magic now does not mean you have to whip your wands out for everything!"

—Molly Weasley, *Harry Potter and the Order of the Phoenix*

Molly Weasley was perhaps the fiercest mother in the wizarding world. A brave witch with a flair for problem-solving, Molly and her husband, Arthur, were members of the Order of the Phoenix during the First Wizarding War . . . despite the fact that she was already raising seven children before the war would run its course.

Molly and Arthur raised their children well, with many of them becoming talented dragon experts, successful shop owners, and high-level officials within the Ministry of Magic.

Molly Weasley was a tigress in the face of danger. She was quite instrumental to Harry and the Order's survival during the Second Wizarding War. Fortifying her home with spells and enchantments, she opened it to any in the Order and was always willing to provide protection, a meal, and a warm bed to those supporting the cause.

Prior to the Battle of Hogwarts, Molly stood at Professor McGonagall's side to cast protective enchantments around Hogwarts. And of course, it was Molly Weasley who dueled and ultimately killed the notorious Death Eater Bellatrix Lestrange, Lord Voldemort's most dedicated and vicious follower.

Narcissa Malfoy

CUNNING · GUARDED · POISED

"The Dark Lord himself forbade me to speak of this."

—Narcissa Malfoy, *Harry Potter and the Half Blood Prince*

Although not a Death Eater herself, Narcissa Malfoy was often surrounded by Death Eaters, including her older sister, Bellatrix Lestrange; her husband, Lucius Malfoy; and her son, Draco. But beyond her association with the Dark Lord, Narcissa was a loving mother who doted on her son, with a cunning mind well suited to protecting her interests.

After Lucius was sent to Azkaban for his role in the battle at the Department of Mysteries, the Dark Lord set Draco to do the near-impossible task of murdering Albus Dumbledore. In *Harry Potter and the Half-Blood Prince*, Narcissa sought out Severus Snape and convinced him to make an Unbreakable Vow to aid Draco on his mission. She then escorted Draco to Borgin and Burkes, where she helped him obtain a Vanishing Cabinet that could be used to smuggle Death Eaters into Hogwarts. After Draco's success, her home was transformed into Lord Voldemort's base of operations.

Narcissa's shining moment, and the act that would ultimately save her family from a lifetime in Azkaban, came in *Harry Potter and the Deathly Hallows – Part 2*. After Lord Voldemort cast the Killing Curse upon Harry, he ordered Narcissa to confirm that the boy was dead. But Narcissa wanted only to be reunited with her son. She quietly asked Harry if Draco was alive, and upon learning that he was, said Harry was dead, so that she and the remaining Death Eaters would go into the castle where she could find her son.

Nymphadora Tonks

CONFIDENT · DEVOTED · FEARLESS

"Don't call me Nymphadora!"
—Nymphadora Tonks, *Harry Potter and the Order of the Phoenix*

Hufflepuffs are known for being kind, patient, loyal, and fair. That's all true, but it doesn't mean they can't also be bold and fearless. One example? Nymphadora Tonks. Though Tonks' mother came from the same family as Bellatrix Lestrange and Narcissa Malfoy, Tonks chose to follow a different path.

The talented Auror was trained by Mad-Eye Moody and was a devoted member of the Order of the Phoenix. As a Metamorphmagus, she could change her appearance at will. (Her hair turned bright red when she was angry.) Aside from the gift's usefulness in her line of duty, in *Harry Potter and the Order of the Phoenix*, she can be seen using it to joke with Hermione and Ginny by making duck and pig faces. During her time in the Order, she fell in love with and married Remus Lupin, and together they had a son named Teddy.

A confident warrior, Tonks was always the first to volunteer for dangerous missions. She escorted Harry to number twelve Grimmauld Place before his fifth year at Hogwarts and volunteered for a similar mission again in *Harry Potter and the Deathly Hallows – Part 1*, in which she protected Ron, who was one of the decoy Harrys. At Christmastime in Harry's sixth year, she defended Harry and the Weasleys against an attack by Bellatrix Lestrange and Fenrir Greyback. She continued to fight for the Order even after her child was born and flew to Hogwarts to defend the school and defeat Lord Voldemort once and for all.

Sadly, Tonks gave up her life in the Battle of Hogwarts.

WOMEN WHO RAN THE WIZARDING WORLD

Many women rose to the top of their professions in the world of witchcraft and wizardry. Here are just a few of them.

Rita Skeeter

AMBITIOUS

"Everyone loves a rebel."

—Rita Skeeter, *Harry Potter and the Goblet of Fire*

The *Daily Prophet* reporter Rita Skeeter was not above sneaky behavior and bending the truth to get a good story, the more sensational the better. Already the biggest name in news by the time Harry and Hermione first met her in *Harry Potter and the Goblet of Fire*, she used her Quick-Quotes Quill to invent answers to her questions.

Rita penned many of *The Daily Prophet* stories that called Harry a liar when he said that Lord Voldemort had returned. She happily reported on the Ministry's witch and wizard hunts after Death Eaters gained control. But she also unknowingly helped Harry and his friends in *Harry Potter and the Deathly Hallows Part – 1* and *2*. Rita's unauthorized biography, *The Life and Lies of Albus Dumbledore*, provided them with clues to Dumbledore's past, which helped them discover that Lord Voldemort was after the Elder Wand.

Madam Rosmerta

ENTERPRISING

"Business would be a lot better if the Ministry wasn't sending Dementors into my pub every other night."

—Madam Rosmerta, *Harry Potter and the Prisoner of Azkaban*

Madam Rosmerta was the owner of the Three Broomsticks pub in Hogsmeade. In addition to running a successful business, Madam Rosmerta was also a close friend and confidante of many of the faculty members at Hogwarts, as well as the former Minister for Magic, Cornelius Fudge.

Madam Rosmerta didn't seem too happy to see Fudge in *Harry Potter and the Prisoner of Azbakan*. She complained that the Dementors the Ministry had sent to Hogwarts and Hogsmeade were putting a serious dent in her business.

Still, the Three Broomsticks remained a favorite spot for students and professors alike to drink Butterbeer and trade in secrets.

Bathilda Bagshot

ACCOMPLISHED

"She's only the most celebrated magical historian of the last century."

—Great-Aunt Muriel, *Harry Potter and the Deathly Hallows – Part 1*

Magical historian Bathilda Bagshot was the author of *A History of Magic*. She was also an old friend of Albus Dumbledore's, having lived in Godric's Hollow, the same village where the Dumbledores once resided.

In *Harry Potter and the Deathly Hallows – Part 1*, Harry learned of Bathilda's connection to Dumbledore from Ron's great-aunt Muriel, who revealed that "she was as close to the Dumbledores as anyone." Bathilda's nephew was the infamous Dark wizard Gellert Grindelwald, who shared a close friendship with Dumbledore when they were young.

While searching for Lord Voldemort's Horcruxes, Harry and Hermione went to Godric's Hollow to talk to her. Bathilda was Rita Skeeter's main source of information for her biography, *The Life and Lies of Albus Dumbledore*.

Unfortunately, Bathilda had been killed by Nagini before Harry and Hermione reached her. Her magical secrets died with her.

Amelia Bones

HONORABLE

Amelia Bones was the Head of the Department of Magical Law Enforcement at the Ministry of Magic. As a high-ranking official, Amelia held a seat on the Wizengamot. She also had an incontrovertible sense of fairness. When Harry was tried in criminal court for doing magic outside of Hogwarts in *Harry Potter and the Order of the Phoenix*, Amelia deposed the witness Arabella Figg.

The Minister for Magic, Cornelius Fudge, as well as Dolores Umbridge and others, dismissed Arabella's testimony and wanted to expel Harry from Hogwarts, but Amelia voted to clear him of all charges. Her honorable behavior in the face of the Minister for Magic inspired others on the council to follow her lead.

Helga Hufflepuff

JUST · LOYAL · HARDWORKING

One of the four founders of Hogwarts School of Witchcraft and Wizardry, Helga Hufflepuff valued loyalty, fairness, and hard work in her students. Hufflepuff house was named for her, and she inspired these same qualities in the many generations of students who were sorted into her house.

Some of the other founders were very selective about the students they were willing to take in their house, including Salazar Slytherin, who wanted to accept only pure-blood students. It is said Helga believed that all magical children were inherently worthy of an education, and this may be part of why Hufflepuff house so values fairness and equality.

In her portrait, Helga is holding a golden cup engraved with her house's symbol, a badger. Lord Voldemort stole the cup and turned it into one of his seven Horcruxes. In *Harry Potter and the Deathly Hallows – Part 2*, Hermione destroyed it with a Basilisk's fang.

Rowena Ravenclaw

Another of the four founders of Hogwarts School of Witchcraft and Wizardry, Rowena Ravenclaw was the most insightful witch of her time. In her students, Rowena valued wit, learning, and wisdom, so the students sorted into Ravenclaw house show these same qualities. But like her great friends Helga Hufflepuff and Godric Gryffindor, Rowena also believed that Hogwarts should be open to all students with magical talents, pure-bloods and Muggle-borns alike.

Both clever and creative, Rowena once owned a beautiful diadem that became quite famous but had been lost for centuries. After Neville led Harry, Hermione, and Ron back to Hogwarts in *Harry Potter and the Deathly Hallows – Part 2*, Luna, a true Ravenclaw, suggested that the diadem might be one of Lord Voldemort's final Horcruxes. Luna led Harry to the ghost of Rowena's daughter—Helena—and eventually to the diadem.

Helena Ravenclaw

LEARNED · PERCEPTIVE · KIND

"I think it's best if you two talk alone. She's very shy."
—Luna Lovegood, *Harry Potter and the Deathly Hallows – Part 2*

Helena Ravenclaw was the daughter of Hogwarts founder Rowena Ravenclaw. As a ghost, she was known as the Grey Lady, and haunted Ravenclaw Tower. Not many knew her as anything other than the Ravenclaw house ghost, but Luna took the time to get to know her.

When Harry told Dumbledore's Army that he was in search of a small artifact related to Hogwarts's history in *Harry Potter and the Deathly Hallows – Part 2*, Luna suggested it might be the Lost Diadem of Ravenclaw. The tiara had been lost for centuries, but Luna thought if he was in search of something that no one alive had seen, then he had best ask someone who was dead.

Helena revealed that another young man had defiled the diadem with Dark magic. She was willing to tell Harry where it was only after he promised to destroy it.

Ariana Dumbledore

SHY · LOVING · DEVOTED

> **"My brother sacrificed many things . . . on his journey to find power, including Ariana."**
> —Aberforth Dumbledore, *Harry Potter and the Deathly Hallows – Part 2*

Ariana Dumbledore, Albus and Aberforth's younger sister, was attacked by three Muggles who saw her doing magic in her youth. From then on, Ariana was unable to do magic or to live a normal life. Her father was sent to Azkaban for killing the three Muggles after he'd learned what they'd done. The family then moved to Godric's Hollow, but Ariana never recovered and died very young. Aberforth said she was very devoted to Albus.

Ariana's portrait hung on the wall in the Hog's Head Inn, which was owned by Aberforth. In *Harry Potter and the Deathly Hallows – Part 2*, Harry, Ron, and Hermione traveled to Hogsmeade, where Aberforth used Ariana's painting to help them sneak into Hogwarts via a secret passage to the Room of Requirement.

GIRLS WHO PROVED THEIR IDEALS ON THE BATTLEFIELD

the Battles at the Burrow

—|— In *Harry Potter and the Half-Blood Prince*, when the Burrow was attacked by Death Eater Bellatrix Lestrange and werewolf Fenir Greyback, Ginny Weasley raced after them in the middle of the night in her bathrobe, trading blows vin a cornfield!

—|— In that same battle, Tonks fought a massive magical fire cast by Bellatrix, then served as Ginny's backup, forcing the evildoers to flee.

—|—One year later, Death Eaters attacked again during Fleur and Bill's wedding reception. While the members of the Order fought, Hemione grabbed Harry and Ron and Apparated. She had already packed a small bag and used an Undetectable Extension Charm on it so they could carry everything they would need for life on the run hunting Horcruxes.

the Battle at the Department of Mysteries

- *Levicorpus!* When cornered and beaten down by a masked Death Eater, Luna sent him flying backward with this defensive spell she learned in a D.A. meeting!

- *Stupefy!* After a Death Eater deflected this spell, Hermione enchanted the thousands of crystal balls shelved in the Department of Mysteries to pelt her attackers.

- *Reducto!* Ginny used this curse on a Death Eater who was approaching the group. Her quick thinking bought the group time until members of the Order—including Tonks—arrived!

the Battle of Hogwarts

- Ginny warned everyone that Severus Snape knew Harry Potter was spotted in Hogsmeade and might be in the castle.

- When Harry confronted Snape in the Great Hall, Minerva McGonagall battled Snape herself, forcing the headmaster from the castle.

- Lord Voldemort told everyone in the castle that if they handed over Harry, they would be safe. Lavender Brown, Cho Chang, Luna Lovegood, Padma Patil, and Parvati Patil all rushed to Harry's side to keep that from happening.

- Molly Weasley and Professor McGonagall cast charms and enchantments to protect the school, buying Harry time to find the Horcrux.

- McGonagall ordered Neville and Seamus to blow up the covered bridge, blocking the Death Eaters from entering.

- Hermione destroyed a Horcrux—Helga Hufflepuff's cup—with a Basilisk fang.

- Hermione stunned Gregory Goyle when he tried to hit Harry with the Killing Curse. Then she hopped on a broom and used her wand to create a hole through the Fiendfyre that engulfed the Room of Requirement.

Porpentina "Tina" Goldstein

DETERMINED · COMPASSIONATE · PRACTICAL

"I've arrested half the people in here."
—Tina Goldstein, *Fantastic Beasts and Where to Find Them*

Tina Goldstein and her sister, Queenie, suffered tragedy at a young age when they lost their parents to dragon pox. The sisters attended Ilvermorny School of Witchcraft and Wizardry in America, where Tina was sorted into Thunderbird house. A driven, practical, capable witch, Tina ultimately rose to become an Auror for the Magical Congress of the United States of America (MACUSA), but she was demoted for attacking a No-Maj (non-magical person) in New York City.

Tina had attacked New Salem Philanthropic Society Leader Mary Lou Barebone after witnessing her beat her adopted son, Credence. Tina couldn't stand by while the young man was hurt. For her actions, Tina was demoted to Wand Permit Officer, working in the dingy basement of MACUSA headquarters. Despite direct orders to leave the NSPS alone, Tina couldn't bring herself to drop her investigation entirely. It was while she was watching Mary Lou give an anti-magic speech that Tina spotted Newt Scamander for the first time, in front of City Bank.

Little did Tina know that her chance run-in with Newt would entangle her in a quest to catch the infamous Dark wizard Gellert Grindelwald and contain his growing movement.

Eleven Times
Tina Took Charge

**"I know what that woman did to you . . .
I know that you've suffered . . . you need to stop this
now . . . Newt and I will protect you."**
—Tina Goldstein, *Fantastic Beasts and Where to Find Them*

1. While Newt was tending to his creatures, Tina presented his case to the International Confederation of Witches and Wizards to prove Newt had unleashed magical creatures in New York.

2. No one knew that the Dark wizard Gellert Grindelwald had infiltrated MACUSA, posing as Percival Graves, Director of Magical Security. By exposing Newt and interfering with the NSPS, Tina interfered in Grindelwald's plans for the Obscurus in New York City.

3. When Tina turned her attention to helping Newt find his missing creatures, she used her connections as an Auror to get information that led them straight to the department store, where the last two beasts Newt needed to recapture, a Demiguise and Occamy, were located.

4. At the department store, Tina caught Newt's Occamy in a teapot.

5. When Grindelwald attempted to corner the Obscurus, who was revealed to be Credence, Tina battled Grindelwald herself, trading blows with him before he escaped.

6. When Newt and Grindelwald cornered Credence in the subway, Tina empathized with the Obscurial, digging into her own personal strength to inspire Credence not to kill both Newt and Grindelwald.

7. After the Obscurus disappeared, Tina seized Grindelwald's wand when he turned on MACUSA Aurors in the subway.

8. Reinstated as Auror, Tina traveled on a solo mission of international importance to Paris in *Fantastic Beasts: The Crimes of Grindelwald.* She successfully tracked down Credence, who had survived and escaped to Europe.

9. Tina was the first to encounter Yusuf Kama, who helped her unravel Credence's identity.

10. At the French Ministry of Magic, Tina defended Newt and helped him bypass security to get to the Records Room.

11. Tina again battled Grindelwald in the cemetery, then lent her power to protect Paris from the Dark wizard's spell.

Queenie Goldstein

KIND • INTUITIVE • CREATIVE

**"I know, I'm sorry, I can't help it.
People are easiest to read when they're hurting."**
—Queenie Goldstein, *Fantastic Beasts and Where to Find Them*

Queenie Goldstein was a gifted Legilimens, which meant that she often read the thoughts of others without trying to, and even at a great distance. She shared an apartment with her older sister, Tina, in New York City and worked in the same Wand Permit Office at MACUSA. But while Tina rose through the ranks to Auror quickly, Queenie spent her workdays "making coffee" and "unjinxing the john."

That was okay for Queenie, though, as she had many creative pursuits outside the office. Queenie loved using her magic to design beautiful clothes, playing with fresh, cover-worthy styles from the *American Charmer*. She had a flair for cooking as well.

Queenie was delighted to meet Newt Scamander and Jacob Kowalski. Jacob was the first No-Maj that Queenie ever had a real conversation with. Queenie couldn't help but be drawn into their adventure.

After Grindelwald was captured, Jacob had his memories erased. Queenie restored them, but when Jacob tried to break up with her over fears MACUSA would arrest her, Queenie put him under a love spell and fled to Paris. Unfortunately, Grindelwald captured Queenie and promised her that she and Jacob could get married in his new world without fear of persecution. Queenie agreed to lend her incredible powers to his evil cause.

Queenie's Five Most Charming Moments

"You're sweet. But we got each other!"
—Queenie Goldstein, *Fantastic Beasts and Where to Find Them*

1. Despite America's strict laws, which separated witches and wizards and No-Majs, Queenie became fast friends with Jacob Kowalski in *Fantastic Beasts and Where to Find Them.*

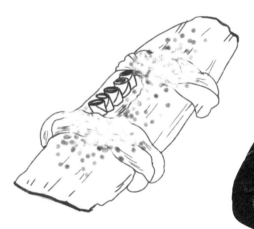

2. While Queenie was at work in the Wand Permit Office, she experienced a powerful stream of thoughts from Tina and learned that her sister and Newt were about to be executed.

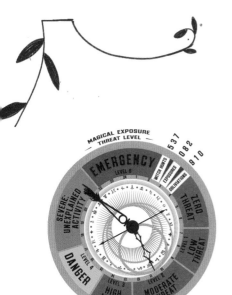

3. Queenie rescued Jacob from being Obliviated by turning her Legilimency skills against one of her coworkers.

4. After retrieving Newt's case with Jacob, Queenie smuggled Newt, Tina, and Jacob out of MACUSA in Newt's case.

5. When she saw Leta Lestrange's picture inside Newt's shed, Queenie used her mind-reading skills to lend Newt some advice about love saying, "She was a taker. You need a giver."

President
Seraphina Picquery

AUTHORITATIVE · STRONG · FAIR

**"I will not be lectured by the man
who let Gellert Grindelwald slip through his fingers."**

—Seraphina Picquery, *Fantastic Beasts and Where to Find Them*

Regal and powerful, Seraphina Picquery was the President of the Magical Congress of the United States of America (MACUSA). In 1927, she dealt with multiple magical threats to the International Statute of Wizarding Secrecy, including an Obscurus, escaped magical creatures, and the Dark wizard Gellert Grindelwald.

At first the president believed the strange happenings to be the work of Grindelwald.

It wasn't until President Picquery saw the Obscurus with her own eyes that the formidable leader came to believe Newt and Tina's claim. But that revelation seemed small next to a much bigger one uncovered in the battle: that Percival Graves was really Gellert Grindelwald in disguise.

After Grindelwald was taken into custody, President Picquery proved how fair she could be when she apologized and thanked Newt and Tina. She even agreed to let Newt free his Thunderbird in New York City to Obliviate all the No-Majs while her staff cleaned up the destruction the Obscurus had caused the city. Much to her credit, President Picquery made good on her promise to Grindelwald and was able to hold him in her custody for some time. Unfortunately, he escaped as soon as he left her watch, while being transferred to Europe to stand trial for his crimes.

MAGICAL EXPOSURE
THREAT LEVEL

EMERGENCY
LEVEL 6

SEVERE:
UNEXPLAINED
ACTIVITY

DANGER
LEVEL 4

HIGH
ALERT
LEVEL 3

MODERATE
LEVEL 2

LOW THREAT
LEVEL 1

ZERO
THREAT

WITCH HUNTS 937
EXPOSURES 088
OBLIVIATIONS 810

Bunty

Bunty was an incredibly dedicated assistant when she worked with Newt in *Fantastic Beasts: The Crimes of Grindelwald*. Bunty worked in Newt's basement, which held a menagerie of injured or displaced creatures in need of help and healing.

Despite the risk to life and limb, Bunty tended to many beasts there, including a family of baby Nifflers. Bunty was also injured from a run-in with Newt's Kelpie, which needed daily treatments. The horselike water creature was quite difficult to tame. Though once bridled, the Kelpie could be docile.

But none of the creatures' mischief or threat of injury bothered Bunty all that much: She was doing what she loved and had the support of a good friend.

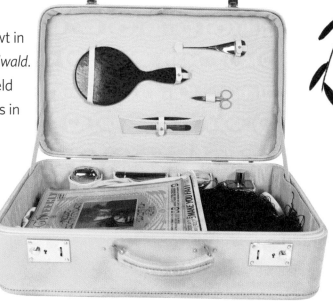

Vinda Rosier

Vinda Rosier was a powerful witch and the closest to Gellert Grindelwald among his acolytes. In *Fantastic Beasts: The Crimes of Grindelwald,* Vinda helped Grindelwald devise a plan to spread information about his movement. She was also present at Grindelwald's massive rally in Paris, where she assisted the Dark wizard in sharing his vision for the world with his followers.

Vinda was instrumental in bringing Queenie Goldstein, a powerful Legilimens, to speak to Grindelwald. The Dark wizard wanted to speak to Queenie to try to sway her to their cause.

Nagini

Nagini was a Maledictus who befriended Credence Barebone while he worked for Skender in the Circus Arcanus. Nagini suffered from a blood curse that caused her to transform into a snake; she was destined to one day take her serpent form forever. She cared deeply for Credence, calling his abilities beautiful and advising him to turn away from Grindelwald, a man who would hunt her kind for sport.

Later in life she joined Lord Voldemort's forces, executing much of the Dark Lord's bidding. Voldemort transferred part of his soul into the snake, who defended him when he was at his most vulnerable. Nagini died during the Battle of Hogwarts, at the hands of Neville Longbottom.

Leta Lestrange

PROUD • INTELLIGENT • SELF-RELIANT

**"Regret is my constant companion, Leta.
Do not let it become yours."**

—Albus Dumbledore, *Fantastic Beasts: The Crimes of Grindelwald*

Leta Lestrange was a gifted witch, born from an ancient and powerful pure-blood wizarding family. At a young age Leta was involved in a shipwreck where she lost her younger brother, Corvus. She blamed herself for the incident her entire life—her Boggart even took the shape of the heartbreaking scene.

At Hogwarts, Leta befriended a young Newt Scamander after she found him caring for creatures including a raven chick. He opened up her world to the beauty of magical beasts, including a tree filled with Bowtruckles.

In *Fantastic Beasts: The Crimes of Grindelwald*, Leta was looking forward to a happier future. She was working for the Ministry of Magic and was engaged to Newt's brother, Theseus. But the past refused to stay buried, as rumors swirled that an ancient prediction pointed to the return of her brother.

After revealing that Credence Barebone was not Corvus Lestrange, Leta attended Grindelwald's rally in Paris. Grindelwald invited Leta to join his side, but she refused, heroically attacking him and destroying the apparatus he used for his visions. She was last seen consumed by the flames Grindelwald had cast.

Four More Notable Women

Irma Dugard was once a servant to the Lestrange family in *Fantastic Beasts: The Crimes of Grindelwald*. She had traveled to America with Leta and her younger brother, Corvus, as children to protect them from Yusuf Kama. Credence Barebone sought her out in her seamstress shop for answers about his family, but she was killed by the bounty hunter Gunnar Grimmson.

Slytherin student Pansy Parkinson was one of Harry Potter's loudest critics at Hogwarts. Just before the Battle of Hogwarts, Lord Voldemort sent a message to everyone at the school that if they turned over Harry Potter, he would not harm them. Pansy was the first to point at Harry and say, "What are you waiting for? Someone grab him!" That prompted Professor McGonagall to send the entire Slytherin contingent to the dungeon.

Gryffindor student Romilda Vane developed a crush on Harry in *Harry Potter and the Half-Blood Prince*. Inspired by Potions class, where Professor Slughorn introduced them to Amortentia, Romilda brewed the love potion and left it in a box of chocolates in Harry's dormitory room. Unfortunately for all involved, Ron spotted them first! Poor Romilda never got her man, but she did join Dumbledore's Army and fought bravely in the Battle of Hogwarts.

Arabella Figg was a Squib, or a person of magical parentage with no magical abilities. She lived in the Dursleys' neighborhood in Little Whinging and often looked out for Harry. In *Harry Potter and the Order of the Phoenix*, Arabella came to Harry's aid when he stood trial for casting a Patronus Charm in front of a Muggle outside of school. Arabella's witness testimony helped clear the young wizard's name of all charges.